# Mr. Jeremy Fisher

FREDERICK WARNE
Published by the Penguin Group
Penguin Books Ltd, 27 Wrights Lane, London W8 5TZ, England
Penguin Putnam Inc., 375 Hudson Street, New York, NY 10014, USA
Penguin Books Australia Ltd, Ringwood, Victoria, Australia
Penguin Books Canada Ltd, 10 Alcorn Avenue, Toronto, Ontario, Canada M4V 3B2
Penguin Books (N.Z.) Ltd, Private Bag 102902, NSMC, Auckland, New Zealand

Penguin Books Ltd, Registered Offices: Harmondsworth, Middlesex, England

Visit our web site at: www.peterrabbit.com

First published by Frederick Warne 2000
1 3 5 7 9 10 8 6 4 2

Copyright © Frederick Warne & Co., 2000
Illustrations from *The World of Peter Rabbit and Friends*<sub>TM</sub> animated television and video series,
a TV Cartoons Ltd production for Frederick Warne & Co., copyright © Frederick Warne & Co., 1993

ISBN 0 7232 4616 5

Printed and bound in Singapore by Tien Wah Press (Pte) Ltd

# Mr. Jeremy Fisher

From the authorized animated series based on the original tales

## BY BEATRIX POTTER™

### FREDERICK WARNE

Once upon a time there was a frog called Mr. Jeremy Fisher. He lived in a little damp house amongst the buttercups at the edge of a pond.

Mr. Jeremy Fisher looked out of his window one morning and was very pleased to see large drops of rain. 'I will get some worms and go fishing and catch a dish of minnows for my tea,' he said. 'If I catch more than five fish, I will invite my friends Mr. Alderman Ptolemy and Sir Isaac Newton.'

Mr. Jeremy Fisher dug up some fine worms to use as bait.

Then he put on a macintosh and a pair of shiny goloshes.

He set off with enormous hops towards
his boat—a round, green lily-leaf
in the middle of the pond.

Using a reed pole, Mr. Jeremy pushed the boat out into open water. 'I know a good place for minnows,' he said.

Mr. Jeremy Fisher sat for nearly an hour with the rain trickling down his back, but there was no sign of any minnows.

'This is getting tiresome; I think I should like some lunch,'
he said. 'I will eat a butterfly sandwich and wait until
the shower is over.'

While Mr. Jeremy was enjoying his lunch, a great big water-beetle came up underneath the lily-leaf and tweaked the toe of one of his goloshes.

'What a nuisance! I think I had better get away from here.'
he said, shoving the boat away a little and dropping in his bait.

Underneath his boat lurked
an enormous trout!

It seized Mr. Jeremy with a
snap—'Ow! Ow! Ow!'

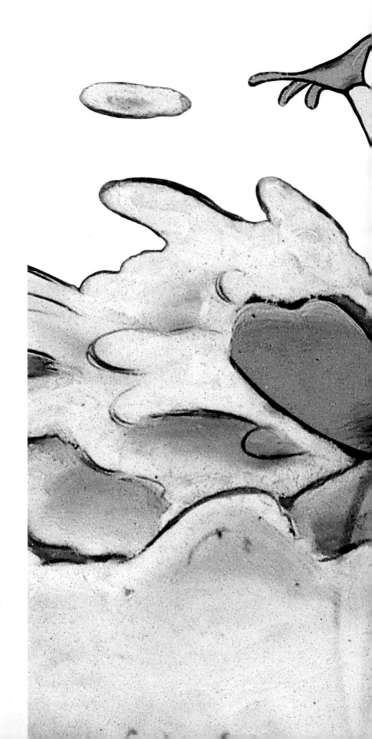

Luckily, the trout was so
displeased with the taste of
the macintosh that in less
than half a minute it spat him
out again. It did, however,
swallow the goloshes.

Mr. Jeremy swam with all his might to the edge of the pond and scrambled up the bank feeling very shaken.

'I have lost my rod and basket; but it does not much matter,' he said, 'for I am sure I shall never dare to go fishing again!'

Mr. Jeremy waited for his friends to arrive. He could not offer them fish, but he had something else in his larder.

Sir Isaac wore his black and gold waistcoat.
And Mr. Alderman Ptolemy brought a
salad with him in a string bag.

Instead of a nice dish of minnows, they had roasted grasshopper with lady-bird sauce, which is a lovely treat for frogs!